# Bob's Secret Hideaway

Written by Tom Dickinson
Illustrated by Jimothy Oliver

## Collins

Bob had a secret hideaway,
that only he would know.

2

He crept up there alone at night,
to watch the moonlight glow.

Then Bob invited all his friends,
but all they brought was noise.

So Bob decided not to share,
his treehouse or his toys.

Now Bob was left alone again,
in his treehouse feeling sad.

He found his secret was no fun,
without the friends he had.

He heard a knock upon the door,
and opened it a crack.

11

He peeped outside and happily saw,
that his friends had all come back!

# Bob's hideaway

# Ideas for reading

Written by Clare Dowdall, PhD
*Lecturer and Primary Literacy Consultant*

**Learning objectives:** read words containing taught GPCs and –s, –es, –ing, –ed, –er and –est endings; read other words of more than one syllable that contain taught GPCs; checking that the text makes sense to them as they read and correcting inaccurate reading; making inferences on the basis of what is being said and done; discussing the significance of the title and events

**Curriculum links:** Art and Design

**High frequency words:** had, but, it, for, that, only, he, would, there, night, then, all, friends, they, was, so, toys, now, again, found, saw, come

**Interest words:** hideaway, know, alone, watch, moonlight, invited, brought, noise, decided, treehouse, alone, without, heard, knock, upon, opened, peeped, outside

**Resources:** paper, pencils

**Word count:** 93

## Getting started

- Read the title together and look at the cover illustration. Ask children to discuss what a hideaway is and to describe Bob's hideaway, using the picture to support their ideas.

- Encourage children to describe their own secret hiding places or favourite places to play, supporting and developing their vocabulary choices.

- Read the blurb aloud together. Ask children to suggest why Bob's hideaway doesn't stay a secret for long and predict what might happen in the poem.

- Introduce the interest words that feature in this poem. Focus on strategies for reading words that are built from two known words, e.g. *hide-away*, *moon-light*, and words that have familiar endings, e.g. *invite-d*, *decide-d*, *peep-ed*.

## Reading and responding

- Explain that this story is written as a poem. Read pp2–3 to the children, emphasising the rhythm and rhyme. Ask children to read these pages aloud with you to practise reading with fluency and expression.